Aunt Esmerelda is Peter's favorite aunt. She loves colorful things, and she's got her eye on Grandma's costume...and Grandma's striped dress, Grandma's pink pearl necklace, and Grandma's yellow purse too.

Uncle Charlie loves adventure. He's staying home for Grandma's birthday celebration, but he's going on a safari nevertheless.

Can you help Grandma find her rainbow costume in time for the party? Let's go!

In each picture you can find: Peter, Percy, Gobble, Grandma, Uncle Charlie, and Aunt Esmerelda. Keep an eye out for Peter's favorite aunt! If you find her, you'll find all of the parts of Grandma's costume. Look carefully and have fun!

Originally published as *Poldi und Paulchen*, © Christian Jeremies and Fabian Jeremies, 2014, by Baumhaus Verlag, an imprint of Bastei Lübbe AG.

Published by Sourcebooks Jabberwocky, an imprint of Sourcebooks, Inc.
P.O. Box 4410, Naperville, Illinois 60567-4410
(630) 961-3900
Fax: (630) 961-2168
www.sourcebooks.com

Library of Congress Cataloging-in-Publication data is on file with the publisher.

Source of Production: Leo Paper, Heshan City, Guangdong Province, China
Date of Production: August 2015
Run Number: 5004261

Printed and bound in China.
LEO 10 9 8 7 6 5 4 3 2 1

The BIG Penguin PARTY

with Peter and Percy

Christian and
Fabian Jeremies

sourcebooks
jabberwocky

Today is Grandma's 90th birthday, and everyone's here to celebrate! Peter is excited for the big costume party tonight.

"Where did I put my striped dress?"

thinks Grandma. Just then—ding dong—the doorbell rings. "Hello, I'm Percy. This letter was left in our mailbox, but I think it's for you."

"Oh, a letter from the mayor!" exclaims Grandma.
"What does it say?" Peter asks.
"He wants to come by this evening and congratulate me," says Grandma. "He's bringing a photographer, but I haven't found everything for my costume yet!

Where are my green stockings?"

"We'll help you look!" says Peter.
Percy agrees, nodding enthusiastically.

"My other stocking must be here somewhere,"

says Grandma, heading into the living room.
"I don't like stockings," says Peter, scratching his shin.
"I do, especially green ones!" Percy replies. The little crocodile looks
in the teakettle, but the stocking isn't there. Where could it be?!

"If I only knew
where my pink pearl necklace was,"

Grandma murmurs, looking around the balcony in confusion.
Percy looks behind every flowerpot, and Peter sticks his head
between the daisies.
"Achoo!" he sneezes, and again: "Aaachoooo!"
"Bless you!" says Aunt Esmerelda.

"My blue scarf is still missing,"

says Grandma, lifting up a corner of the carpet.
"It was on the piano yesterday," says Peter. Now three little
penguins sit there, listening to Uncle Herbert tap the keys.
"Owww, that's too loud!" complain Peter and Percy.

"My hat with the peacock feather must be up here,"

says Grandma, out of breath from climbing the stairs.
"Probably in the attic," whispers Percy, trembling a
little. "It's swarming with bats and ghosts..."
"Bat-ghosts?" giggles Peter.
Together, they brave the stairs.

"Now I need my red gloves—
then I'll almost be wearing enough colors to impress the mayor!"
Peter looks behind the books. Percy checks inside a lamp shade.
"Click!" says Uncle Willy, and he turns on the light.

"Your bright-yellow purse
would be great in the picture,"
says Peter.

"You're right!" exclaims Grandma. "I just washed it."
Percy climbs in the washing machine to look.
"It's nice of you to help," Peter whispers to him.
"I love to help!" says Percy, grinning.

"My purple shoes are still missing!

I can't be photographed in just socks! Do you see them anywhere?" asks Grandma.
"Maybe they're in the soup bowl?" suggests Peter.
"Or under the table?" Percy chimes in.

"Oh my, so late already? Children, hurry up! You
need to get ready!" calls Grandma.

"I can find my orange coat by myself."

"But I don't have a costume yet," Percy whispers to Peter.
"Don't worry, I'm sure we can find something for you in my
room," answers Peter.

"Look here," says Peter, taking a big box out of the corner of his room. They dig through the box until there is a mountain of costumes, hats, and scarves on the floor.

"This one's great!"

Percy calls out.

"Happy Birthday!" says the Mayor, congratulating Grandma.

"Everyone has a wonderful costume, especially you!" he
says as he kisses her hand.
"All that searching was worth it in the end!" says Grandma,
smiling into the camera.
"And it was so much fun!" cheer Peter and Percy.

Peter feels great in his costume. Finally, he's big and tall! He's even happier about his new friend, Percy. He can't wait to invent things and go on adventures with him.

Gobble thinks Peter's relatives are great because they always make such a mess. But he likes the photographer the best—he's never seen such a big ladybug before.

Percy loves his dog costume so much that he never wants to take it off. It even makes him feel more courageous.

Grandma's birthday party is a real hit! Her costume makes her look at least 50 years younger.